Dear Parent:

Congratulations! Your child is taking the first steps on an exciting journey. The destination? Independent reading!

STEP INTO READING® will help your child get there. The program offers books at five levels that accompany children from their first attempts at reading to reading success. Each step includes fun stories, fiction and nonfiction, and colorful art. There are also Step into Reading Sticker Books, Step into Reading Math Readers, and Step into Reading Phonics Readers— a complete literacy program with something to interest every child.

Learning to Read, Step by Step!

Ready to Read **Preschool–Kindergarten**
• **big type and easy words** • **rhyme and rhythm** • **picture clues**
For children who know the alphabet and are eager to begin reading.

Reading with Help **Preschool–Grade 1**
• **basic vocabulary** • **short sentences** • **simple stories**
For children who recognize familiar words and sound out new words with help.

Reading on Your Own **Grades 1–3**
• **engaging characters** • **easy-to-follow plots** • **popular topics**
For children who are ready to read on their own.

Reading Paragraphs **Grades 2–3**
• **challenging vocabulary** • **short paragraphs** • **exciting stories**
For newly independent readers who read simple sentences with confidence.

Ready for Chapters **Grades 2–4**
• **chapters** • **longer paragraphs** • **full-color art**
For children who want to take the plunge into chapter books but still like colorful pictures.

STEP INTO READING® is designed to give every child a successful reading experience. The grade levels are only guides. Children can progress through the steps at their own speed, developing confidence in their reading, no matter what their grade.

Remember, a lifetime love of reading starts with a single step!

For two great dentists:
Barry J. Cunha and Brenda J. Nishimura
—S.K.

Text copyright © 1999 by Stephen Krensky.
Illustrations copyright © 1999 by Hideko Takahashi.
All rights reserved under International and Pan-American Copyright Conventions. Published in the United States by Random House Children's Books, a division of Random House, Inc., New York, and simultaneously in Canada by Random House of Canada Limited, Toronto.

www.stepintoreading.com

Educators and librarians, for a variety of teaching tools, visit us at www.randomhouse.com/teachers

Library of Congress Cataloging-in-Publication Data
Krensky, Stephen.
My loose tooth / by Stephen Krensky ; illustrated by Hideko Takahashi.
   p.   cm. — (Step into reading. A step 2 book)
SUMMARY: A young child describes in rhyme what it's like to have a loose tooth.
ISBN 0-679-88847-0 (pbk.) — ISBN 0-679-98847-5 (lib. bdg.)
[1. Teeth—Fiction. 2. Stories in rhyme.]
I. Takahashi, Hideko, ill.   II. Title.   III. Step into reading. Step 2 book.
PZ8.3.K869   My   2003   [E]—dc21   2002013449

Printed in the United States of America   19 18 17 16 15 14 13 12 11

STEP INTO READING, RANDOM HOUSE, and the Random House colophon are registered trademarks of Random House, Inc.

STEP INTO READING®

STEP 2

MY LOOSE TOOTH

by Stephen Krensky
illustrated by Hideko Takahashi

Random House 🏠 New York

4

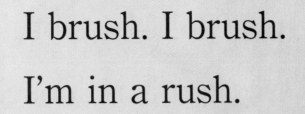

I brush. I brush.

I'm in a rush.

Oh, no! My tooth!
My tooth is loose!

My other teeth
are still stuck tight.
My other teeth
still like to bite.

My loose tooth moves.

It twists around.

Back and forth
and up and down.

Should I stop
my crunchy crunching?
Should I stick to
mushy munching?

Do lions have
this problem, too?

What do sharks and
hippos do?

I smile.

I frown.

I growl.

I stare.

My tooth stays loose.

It's just not fair.

I want it out!
And then, you'll see,
the tooth fairy
will visit me.

I hop around
on just one foot.

I get tired—
my tooth stays put!

And then one day, while I'm at lunch…

My tooth ends up
in what I munch!

"Hooray! Hooray!
Hooray!" I shout.
"My tooth! My tooth!
It's finally out!"

29

There is a hole
in my mouth now.
It will fill up.
Do you know how?

A brand-new tooth
will take its place.
A brand-new part
of my old face!